Rosie's Wonderful Dances

Also by Lyndsay Thwaites
SUPER ADAM AND ROSIE WONDER

ROSIE'S WONDERFUL DANCES
A CORGI BOOK 0 552 522686

PRINTING HISTORY
Andre Deutsch Ltd hardcover edition published 1984
Corgi edition published 1985

Corgi Books are published by
Transworld Publishers Ltd.
Century House
61-63 Uxbridge Road
Ealing, London W5 5SA

Printed in Belgium by Casterman s.a.

Rosie's Wonderful Dances

LYNDSAY THWAITES

CORGI BOOKS

One afternoon Rosie felt in a dancing mood. She dressed herself in her new pink dancing dress and her dancing shoes. Mum put on a record. It was Rosie's favourite.

The music was light and sparkling. Rosie thought of a beautiful garden. 'I think I'll be a flower,' she said and curled herself up into a flower bud. Then she slowly unfolded her petals. The blue flower danced in the breeze and sang in the sunshine. A butterfly came to visit her. 'This is my favourite dance,' said Rosie.

Soon the music changed and it became bouncy and bright. Rosie thought of the clowns she had seen at the circus and on the T.V. She began to tumble all around the room. 'I am a funny fall-about clown with a big red nose. I can juggle three balloons with my toes – and all the other clowns are my friends.'

Then the door opened. Adam was home from school and he was tired and grumpy. 'You look stupid,' he said, and went to get something to eat.

Rosie was cross. 'I would like to tie Adam up and scare him,' she said. She crouched down and danced a slow, creepy, crawly sort of spidery dance. 'I am a big fat hairy spider with four arms and four legs and I would like a mean little boy for my dinner.'

The door opened. It was Adam again and he felt much better. 'I'd like to dance, too, Rosie,' he said. 'I've got some good ideas.'

'OK, if you're in a good mood now,' said Rosie, 'but I don't want you treading on my feet or getting in the way.'

The music changed again – it became very fast and loud.
Adam began to stamp his feet and shake his arms about.
  'Listen, it sounds just like our old washing machine,'
he shouted. 'Come on, let's do a washing machine dance.'
  Rosie and Adam bumped and shook themselves all
around the room. It was a very good dance.

Suddenly the door opened and in came their sister, Kitty.

'I am trying to do my homework and you are making an awful row!' she said crossly. 'You sound like two big elephants jumping up and down.'

'We're only dancing, Kitty,' Rosie and Adam said. 'If you like we'll do a quiet one now.'

Kitty went out and they started to dance again. But the music wasn't very quiet. It grew louder and louder. It filled the room – it sounded like a thunderstorm. Boom Boom Boom!

'I am the lightning that flashes through the sky!' yelled Rosie.

'I am the thunder. I stamp around in the clouds with my big boots on and frighten everybody!' yelled Adam.

They made a lot of noise.

The door opened again and Dad stood there with Thomas on his shoulders.

'What's going on?' he asked. 'I thought the roof was falling in.'

'It's our thunder and lightning dance, Dad,' they shouted.

'Well, try a quieter one,' said Dad. 'Kitty is trying to work. How about a nice peaceful fine weather dance?' and he went off to read his newspaper.

Luckily the music did change. It became slow and gentle and dreamy. Rosie thought of little clouds on a fine summer's day. She lifted her arms and legs slowly and danced a floating fluffy cloud dance. She was a little white cloud, floating in the sky, quietly singing a sleepy song.

Mum popped her head around the door. 'It's tea-time, you dreamy dancers,' she called, 'and hurry up because Thomas is about to start on the buns.'

Rosie and Adam sat down to eat but they didn't stop pretending. Rosie pretended to be a messy monster, and Adam was a silly big bird, pecking at his plate. Mum and Dad soon got cross.

'This is no place for monsters and silly big birds,' said Dad. 'Go and play upstairs until bedtime.'

Rosie lay on her bed with her eyes closed and waved her arms and legs in the air. 'I'm in my space glider and I'm going to visit the man in the moon.'

'Well, I'm in my Superfast Space Rocket,' said Adam. 'I'm going to the moon, too, and I bet I get there first!'

'Bet you don't,' said Rosie. 'My glider is magic. See you later!'